When you draw the stone from the water, the stone drips.
When you draw the water from the stone, the stone cracks.
And through the cracks in the stone, a breath of spirit
To stoke the flames within the stone.

ISBN 978-1-63784-883-8 (paperback)
ISBN 978-1-63784-884-5 (digital)

Copyright © 2025 by Brenden Haukos

All rights reserved. No part of this publication may be reproduced, distributed, or transmitted in any form or by any means, including photocopying, recording, or other electronic or mechanical methods without the prior written permission of the publisher. For permission requests, solicit the publisher via the address below.

Hawes & Jenkins Publishing
16427 N Scottsdale Road Suite 410
Scottsdale, AZ 85254
www.hawesjenkins.com

Printed in the United States of America

Pit FC

BRENDEN HAUKOS

Pit FC 1

A fight is alive.

Enter into the living, breathing glory. This is you at your savage core. Pit FC 1 is here, and the action is live.

The Pit waits. The Pit breathes. A shadow of the ever-departing present casts over all our barbaric souls. Your soul was forged in the elemental furnace of vast and intense conflict. Water may quench fire; earth may absorb water. Always according to the instance.

In this instance, it was Two Hawks vs. Whirlwind Dervish that set the stage for all that is to come. At this moment, perchance, the success of Pit FC waited in the balance of their performance.

As the battle began, Two Hawks ran to the center of the Pit and crept down into a crouch, his hands held up in a tight guard. In his dreams, he became two hawks and could fly. The sound of a strange keening echoed around the Pit.

Whirlwind Dervish appeared to fly as he sprinted around the Pit's circular wall. Dervish descended upon Two Hawks still circling. He struck him with a roundhouse kick to the leg and, spinning, a backfist at the head.

Two Hawks ducked the strike. He captured the opposite arm and sent Dervish, end over end, with his own momentum, onto the clay ground. They both sprang to their feet, Two Hawks still controlling Dervish's wrist. Two Hawks stepped in to trip, but Dervish's balance was too good, and he spun free. Yet, instead of escaping, he cut back in out of nowhere with a sharp elbow to the brow. Blood gushed down into Two Hawks's right eye.

In that moment, Two Hawks stood with his left hand tight to his left temple and his right arm swinging at an absent target while Whirlwind Dervish lunged forward, his chin tucked back, his left arm extended back, and his right elbow knifing into Two Hawks's brow. A one-of-a-kind NFT of this moment was minted by the production team and sold anonymously three weeks later at auction for $12,000.

The heart of fighting is the play between resilience and attrition, between one's skill and another's toughness, with the mirror looking back through you. Sweat stings your eyes as it flows past. In this instance, it is blood.

PIT FC

Two Hawks came back like a flutter of wings—the black gleam of an impossible blade. Of the eight fighters in Pit FC, Two Hawks was magic. He could do the impossible in impossible ways. Half blind and maybe fully blind in trance, Two Hawks rose to a level where Whirlwind Dervish could not follow. The barrage of straight strikes that followed displayed a relentless ferocity that was truly unnatural. Dervish buckled, then broke. Two Hawks stood above Whirlwind Dervish, raining down heavy blows. When the storm was over, he stopped, then stepped back.

Whirlwind Dervish did not rise. Two Hawks raised up his arms in victory. He went over to Dervish and knelt beside him. They clasped hands. Two Hawks cupped Dervish's head in his hand and whispered something to him. Dervish nodded. Their moment passed, and they left the Pit.

The interviewer introduced him to the audience: "Two Hawks, still undefeated, 14–0. This latest victory came over a friend and former training partner. Just how hurt were you?"

"Oh, the elbow? Yeah, he split me open. I was never so badly hurt that I couldn't remember who I am or what I have always done. To be here in the moment, still undefeated: this is what I live for."

"Was there anything Dervish did that surprised you?"

"The elbow. Haha. But no, really, it was his directness that surprised me. I didn't think he had that in him. We went on to see that I am levels above Whirlwind, in the area of directness."

"What's next for Two Hawks?"

"Dmitri Petrovich is fighting Artemeli Skryke in the final bout. I want the winner."

"Lastly, can you share with us what you said to Whirlwind Dervish after the fight?"

"I'm not going to share. Those words were for Dervish alone. This is respectful, I think. Right?"

*****

Hijinks Olsen stared across the Pit at Juniper Jinn. The camera hovered on his face, barely obscured by bright yellow paint. He had short sandy-blonde hair above a slightly sagging brow and a pair of narrow blue eyes, gleaming luridly with a somewhat demented glint. Improbably circular dimples framed his mouth, smiling in anticipation.

The camera cut to an upward angle, framing his whole body as he paced back and forth, his gaze still fixed on Jinn, throwing his arms down from the elbow, flexing and loosening up. His hips turned smoothly from left to right and back. The lingering view allowed the audience to study the contender in an aura of indeterminacy, a judgment postponed.

Besides the yellow face paint, this pale figure of menace wore emerald green spandex leggings. The overall impression was one of moderate strength and awkward potential. He was rigid in his trunk, but his legwork suggested something more fluid and uncanny. The viewer looked closer, and the demented look was gone—in its place was concentrated zeal.

Juniper Jinn, the lone female fighter among Pit FC's eight combatants, was jibing Olsen with obscenities. She went down into a pistol, stood up, and did the other side. She was 5'7" and a jungle of muscle. By all appearances, she would be the more explosive athlete, next to the lankier 6'0" Olsen. She wore her raven hair in the mark of a true savage: unbound, draped over her shoulders, and a third of the way down her back. Either she was indifferent to getting her hair pulled or she mocked her opponent with brash confidence.

She wore short black spandex shorts, black nipple pasties, and sported a crimson red scar painted diagonally across her face. She tumbled over her shoulder, rolling to her feet, from side to side. She rolled her ankles. She looked up at the sky, then back to her opponent. The live feed cut to an overhead shot as the fighters advanced to the center of the ring, both fighters in a conventional stance, and the distance between them closed.

Hijinks circled right along the edge of the pit. Juniper turned toward him, bobbing, her guard on her chin and forehead, elbows flared. Circling away, then cutting back toward the center—Hijinks darted at her with a flurry of straights, switching through his stances. The third shot connected with Juniper's left orbital, sending her back a single step. She continued to jaw him.

Olsen closed the distance, locking up the clinch around her neck, trying to bully her back against the clay wall while kneeing her middle. She exploded through his clinch, butting him in the head with an upward thrust. Two streaking lines of fresh blood materialized on Juniper's forehead, intersecting at the nose and blending with the red paint. Now we saw Olsen. He spat a wad of blood, then bared a wide, toothless smile. His front teeth were gone, embedded in Jinn's forehead.

Olsen clinched her by the back of her neck and kneed her in the gut again. Jinn came back with a one-two jab-cross, each strike punctuated with a shrill "Ya!" but came up empty, then found her range with the up kick to the balls that was the signature of her style. He ate the direct hit as if it were nothing. She laughed a single, mirthless laugh.

Jinn circled left. Olsen stepped out of range of Jinn's check right hook, then cut back in with the cross. Jinn hadn't seen the strike coming, and she was caught off-balance. She stumbled back, bracing herself against the wall, her vision blurred—but not so much that she didn't see the—and she escaped the flying knee, dashing off to the right.

They moved back into the center of the Pit, and from above we saw as Jinn threw a couple of shots to the liver and lower abdomen, then came up against his chin with an elbow. Juniper Jinn dipped into the body lock, loaded him up on her hip, and slammed him sideways into the clay. She bounced back up and backed off a step, goading him back to his feet.

He hip-heisted himself up, then switched to southpaw, advancing with three consecutive jabs and chasing her with the right hand. He was breathing heavily now through his mouth. He threw again, a front kick to the body, which was blocked.

Olsen cut off her escape, but Jinn pivoted and escaped back the other way. She screamed with each strike she threw, landing an inside-leg kick on his lead leg. He promptly switched stances, carving across the space with the lead left double-jab, then a right cross, then a switch-kick to the head as she tried to escape again to the right. The kick landed flush, and though her head bounced off her shoulder and was subsequently yanked the other way as Olsen had to rip his foot free of her hair, she barked a shriek of pain, then went back to jawing him.

He flashed his broken grin.

She came back with a pawing jab to the body that was mostly deflected.

Next, Olsen threw the fateful kick. Jinn's knee popped in at impact, and she let out a puff of air. In the instant that proved so critical, she fell forward and launched herself off her remaining foot into a powerful double-leg takedown, bowling Olsen over onto his back. With a quick knee to the groin, she scrambled past his guard, wrapping up a head-and-arm choke. Olsen wouldn't tap.

When he opened his eyes, Juniper Jinn was leaning over him to plant a friendly peck on his forehead.

In the dusky antechamber, the interviewer tried to capture her initial reaction: "Any thoughts after a statement victory like that?"

"I can kick your ass, and I can kick your boyfriend's ass too. I'm a free woman, and I'm not going anywhere. Olsen, I love you, but you fight like a chump. L3B, give me some real meat! I want Warhole Eleven next!" She was standing with the aid of crutches.

"That was an amazing finish, to come back after the injury. What motivates you to fight like that?"

"Knowing that I'll never have children of my own, I'm living the legend for myself. Juniper Jinn, the legend."

"Who do you perceive as your biggest threat moving forward in the Pit Fight Championship?"

"It's either Warhole Eleven or Two Hawks. Maybe Artemeli—he's the dark horse."

"Who do you perceive as your hottest potential hookup?"

"Again, Two Hawks...or Artemeli. Definitely not Warhole Eleven."

"Good luck in your next fight."

Jinn fist-bumped the interviewer.

*****

Up next with the interviewer was Pickup Truck Huck, here for a prefight chat before his bout with Warhole Eleven. He stood more than two heads above the interviewer. The words "Candy Ass" tattooed across his chest were blurred out in the live feed.

"How do you address your previous four losses to Warhole Eleven?"

"I've known a lot of folks to say he beats me nine out of ten times. To my reckoning, the one out of ten chance could be about to hit. I don't think that just because he beat me four times by KO, he has as much advantage as he is credited with. Remember, all you good hardworking folk out there, this is the Huck show, and the star of the show is yours truly."

"What if you lose?"

"I will never ask for a rematch again. It's in the contract. Signed in blood."

"Are all the Pit FC contracts signed in blood?"

"All the ones I seen."

Next, the interviewer met briefly with Warhole Eleven. "What is your mindset going into this fight?"

"Huck is that tired ol' ho you don't want to see no mo'. This is in and out, and on to the next one."

"Is it disrespectful of you to look past your opponent like this?"

"A well-deserved disrespect at that."

*****

PIT FC

Warhole showed up in his patented aviator mirror shades. The face-off between 6'6" Warhole Eleven and 6'10" Pickup Truck Huck was epic.

The fight, on the other hand, lasted only eleven seconds. Warhole Eleven knocked him down and then out with hammer fists. The full fight video was the most-viewed clip of Pit FC 1.

The interviewer asked him, "How does it feel to get the W in Pit FC 1?"

"I have mixed reviews, really," Warhole said, chomping on an apple. "After five fights, my legacy is forever linked to this guy, and you can't tell me that that's to my merit."

"It *is* to your merit that you fought and won in the inaugural Pit FC event."

"Thank you."

"What's next for Warhole Eleven?"

"Juniper Jinn looks like she's the real deal. Her skills speak for themselves. I'll be honest. I can't wait to have her mounted."

*****

"As we wait for the main event, we are joined again by undefeated pit fighter Two Hawks. Thanks for joining us. It looks like you're sewn up nicely."

"Thanks, interviewer. It is an honor and a dream fulfilled to be able to showcase my skills at such an amazing event in the history of my sport."

"Let's dive right in: apples or oranges?"

"I don't really care."

"No, really, I was only kidding. But in all seriousness, have you always been the undefeated fighter we see here today, or did you develop out of something baser, like the rest of us?"

"I am always undefeated. But before the day came when I relinquished everything I was not, I was only waiting to be born."

"What has been your secret to dominance?"

"I really think humility is the key to staying on top. If you can't humble yourself to the task at hand, the moment will always be too big for you."

"Do you practice a specific style of fighting or ascribe to any school?"

"I fight to express the ancient grief of this land, to burn brightly in that hot sorrow where winners take damage and losers take losses however they will. When you are alone, that's where I'll find you, and you cannot resist. Whether it be the sub or the knockout, it is there waiting for you."

"Going deep with Two Hawks."

"Thanks again for having me."

PIT FC

"Who do you have in the championship bout?"

"I'm picking Dmitri Petrovich. He's durable, he's proven, and I think he overpowers him."

*****

The fight is life—the light that shines in the darkness. The Pit is violence given a stage and performed. Men and women go to the Pit to participate in the shared love of combat and sport. They have said yes to all that makes one a killer, and that "yes" is every choice he or she ever made.

The Pit swallows all pretension, exuding an exactness of differences revealed. The truth is there for the taking, but no one will let you have it willingly.

Obscurity washes over our days and nights, but in the Pit, that obscurity is scrubbed nearly clean. Doubt and ambivalence are vanquished by the sword of win or lose.

When one steps into the Pit, which has to be dug out of the earth, one steps closer to the heart of gravity. Terrestrial gravitation: not above but below. A cry in the night: for the unadulterated intensities that arise when two bodies go to war. In celestial gravitation, one ascends toward union with God. In the Pit, in terrestrial gravitation, one descends toward uniqueness within the self. In Heaven, all is in communion. In the Pit, one is utterly alone.

No man is any man's equal in the Pit.

No one cared more than these eight fighters, upon whose beings all this fanfare depended. You have to be tough to step into the Pit. You must go with fear, anticipation, and a sense of destiny. You must visualize victory at any cost.

What is the will of the Pit? It is to eradicate all uncertainty in the question of who outdoes who. But this is already one step removed. The will of the Pit is to frame a mutually violent act of struggle against one another, against one's self-made Other.

In the Pit, one is utterly alone.

*****

The interviewer proceeded: "In preparation for tonight's championship bout, we are taking an in-depth look into the minds of each challenger. First, we meet Dmitri Petrovich, undefeated in fifty-four bouts, including seven death matches on the infamous French circuit."

"We are violent beings, and we are sexual beings. But we are also beings of the Word, our very lives delineated by and inscribed with the fonts of our predilections. No other fighter on this roster captures the truth of himself as Word like Dmitri Petrovich. He is an idea, given drive, and made flesh. Brutality as a concept may not have a clear definition, but as a person, it takes perfect form in Dmitri Petrovich. And here he is to meet us. Hello, Dmitri."

"Privyet, interviewer."

"You've had a long, illustrious career. What motivates you to fight?"

"I come from a very poor family of artists and philosophers. I make philosophy with my fist and art with my foot. In honor of Da and Ma."

"If you could impart one thing to any fans you have watching today, what would it be?"

"Eat like champion. Train like champion. Sleep like champion. Breathe like champion. That is all."

"Amazing words."

"Don't ever put your dollar where your heart is."

"Can you elaborate on that last point?"

"Do what drives you, and take no more than you need, and you will not want."

"It sounds as if you are saying something new, although my question was for you to elaborate on what you meant when you said, 'Don't put your dollar where your heart is.'"

"Sounds as if, but it is not. In essence, it's the same."

"Do you have a softer side? What does *woman* mean to you?"

"Woman is the essence of man. In my opinion, there is nothing more perfect or beautiful than woman. Woman gives birth to man, thank God. I must express my gratitude."

"Juniper Jinn celebrates a victory today. How would you feel about facing her?"

"I will fight a woman, but never to the death."

"Does the man who faced death seven times fear it?"

"To fear death is like the infant who fears losing his mother's teat. The little one does not know that the loss might be the first step toward greater independence. I do not fear death, for death will be a great adventure."

"What is the source you go back to?"

"When I was a lad of twelve, I went to a waterfall up in the mountains to make my wish known. I wished to become the most brutal force the world has ever known. Since then, I've been hungry. The full will fall."

"What is the darkest place you have gone to in a fight?"

PIT FC

"I went up against an American wrestler in a death match. The man did not look like much to be in a brawl with me. That said, his pace was relentless and truly exhausting—the way he struck me with one barrage after another, followed by wrestling exchanges he threw in just to tire me out. He would go in on a single and dump me on my butt, only to jump right up. I was wearing out, just standing myself up. His power was nothing, but my power was losing its relevance. And if that wasn't enough to scare me, when I started throwing desperately, he upped the pace another notch. This terrifying crescendo of lethal energy, his name was Bo Wrently, had me questioning who I was or had ever been.

"I had truly met my match. I was going down, and I knew it. My vision was narrowing, getting bleary, my footwork slowing, my explosions losing their explosiveness. I was resigned to meet my maker that day. I wasn't going to beg for mercy.

"I started eating all his shots just to throw back at the air. I had never so much as given up in a workout before that day, but I did give up in that fight.

"As he rained down sulfur on me, I retreated inward, saying goodbye to my memories of Da and Ma, to the memory of my last lover, looking at me over a cup of brewed herbs, the knowing recalcitrance of her gaze, the way she kept everything for herself until the time she would give it all so freely in one great deluge of love, and lastly, I retreated to the awesome place of my training, where I had spent all of my important days, where I then curled up inside myself and cozily drifted off toward…whatever comes next…"

"So what happened?"

"I am still alive."

"How?"

"I always ask myself, 'Why'? Why was I so lucky that, in the last moments, he happened to land a high roundhouse on my elbow and shattered his foot? Why was I spared?

"He collapsed when he brought down the foot. He stood back up but couldn't bear weight on one leg. He held out his hands, as if to fend off a ghost. But his power was all gone. When I look into those eyes, to this day, I see disbelief."

"I am speechless," the interviewer said, then: "What is the most important thing to know in a fight?"

"There are many very important things, but the most important is your breathing. It may be sharp and short or long and wide, depending on the need of the moment. No matter what, the most important thing is that the breath is yours, and you are not its slave."

"And what is your key to victory tonight?"

"I am the better man by twice, and I'm going to prove it."

"If you had to describe yourself in one word, what would it be?"

"Transcendent."

"Love it. Thank you, Dmitri Petrovich."

*****

"Artemeli Skryke is a more difficult man to introduce. He has had no known fights. I'm looking at him right now, and he is a real specimen for a man his stature." The interviewer stuttered over a thirsty laugh. "Let's begin. What are your physical stats?"

"Five feet, six inches. 130 pounds."

"How old are you?"

"Twenty-eight."

"Have you ever been in an actual fight?"

"Not officially. Be assured, I am ready to defend myself tonight."

"How did you prepare for this moment?"

"I am always training, improving my athleticism and acrobatics, as well as my striking and grappling. I am always looking for a new wrinkle to add to my game. Growth is a constant for me. Ten years ago, I was beatable. Today, not so much."

"What are your weaknesses?"

"My size. I give up a lot of weight, and that can be an uphill battle."

"What are your strengths?"

"Everything, really. I'm the Ace."

"Do you have a philosophy of fighting?"

"If you were to watch a fight in reverse, what would you see?"

"I don't know. What?"

"The dissolution of a bond of the most complicated and penetrating nature. A fight is an act of love between two things who have given everything for the love of it."

"Are you more of a striker or a grappler?"

"When you grapple, you seize your first advantage and develop it with each consecutive gesture. That's what I love about grappling."

"How do you get the submission?"

"You have to make your opponent want to give you the sub. Start by offering them something else."

"If you had to describe yourself in one word, what would it be?"

"Tempting."

She had asked her last question, and the intensity and indiscriminability of the moment kept them both paused, each on the verge of asking, "What is that look for?"

He stole away.

"Wait," she cried out.

"What is it?"

"You're the sweetest." She silently wished him luck as she stared into the eyes of his leather dragon mask.

*****

The championship bout was upon us. The live feed had swollen to a viewership of over 2.2 million. There was no crowd, only a lone barn owl looking down from the trees whose interlacing branches obscured a crescent moon in the midsummer sky, yet the atmosphere here was electrifying.

First, we saw Dmitri Petrovich, a mountain, the spine of a continent of a man. He really was a hoss—the male iteration of a Juniper Jinn, muscle on top of muscle. Wing-like lats and jutting quads. His physicality represented strength approaching enormity, and his game was strength weaponized with speed and made indomitable with intelligent coordination.

BRENDEN HAUKOS

No one thought Artemeli Skryke stood a chance. He gave up one hundred twenty pounds and seven inches. Plus, the experience of Dmitri Petrovich was a legend of combat in and of itself. Despite the challenge that stood before him, squeezing his knuckles, Skryke looked, if anything, emboldened. Did those eyes, yielding nothing and not teeming with anything, but just waiting silently, conceal a lack, or did an assassin hide in the night?

Skryke pressed his fist into his palm before him and bowed to his opponent. Petrovich nodded back. The fight commenced.

Dmitri Petrovich advanced across the Pit, southpaw, pumping the right jab into the collapsing space between them. Skryke stabbed him with an oblique kick to the lead knee. Switching stances, Skryke vanished out at an angle and landed an outside leg kick to the thigh.

Petrovich, unhindered, stalked him. He chased Skryke with the lead right hook. Skryke timed his shot as Petrovich was coming in. He failed the second effort on the far leg and had to settle for the single leg. Petrovich offset Skryke's head and sprawled hard, flattening him. As he pressed Skryke's face into the damp clay, Skryke dragged his knees under him, turtling up.

PIT FC

Petrovich captured an arm and used it to wrap up Skryke's neck. Then Petrovich stepped over the hip with his right leg and rolled forward, capturing the leg in the crook of his right arm and setting in a vicious bow-and-arrow choke. Artemeli Skryke, whose neck was flickering with flashing pains, tapped before he was snapped in two.

The interviewer congratulated Dmitri Petrovich on his dominant performance.

"Thank you, miss. I did what I said I would do."

"You are now the Provisional Champion of Pit FC. How does it feel?"

"It feels good."

"Go on and enjoy it."

"Thank you."

Pit FC 2

The next morning, the day of Pit FC 2, Warhole Eleven was the first to rise. He sat in the woods, stinking of DEET, and ate from a satchel of apples. With a wooden dowel that was his allotted personal possession in camp, he worked on his shin conditioning.

Toughness was both a mindset and a practice for Warhole Eleven. While the seven others lay in their cots, Eleven ran hill sprints with a tree bole across his shoulders. He used the same tree for squats, lunges, and overhead presses. He smiled as he pressed through when the reps got hard, exhaling sharply.

He ate heavily, late in the morning, multiple courses—dark leafy green salads, steak, eggs, stir-fried vegetables, yogurt. He flossed and brushed fastidiously. He prayed before bed. He slept on his back under tightly-tucked sheets. He told people, "I meditate on a bed of nails."

PIT FC

The days changed, but Warhole Eleven's disciplines stayed the same. In the afternoon, he split wood and tended a fire, still eating apples and reading the Bible.

Whirlwind Dervish was the second to rise, an hour after Warhole Eleven. He spent long hours in contemplative visualization, not on a bed of nails but on the end of the dock, sitting in a lotus, breathing in a pattern of twenty or more beats with equal pauses between inhalation and exhalation. Iridescent dragonflies flitted by, mating on the breeze.

His head ached from last night's KO. He was haunted by the feeling that there was an impassable chasm between his and Two Hawks's skills, as if the elbow meant nothing at all.

He was able to train for a while, at noon, three hours after matchups were announced. Artemeli Skryke was likely another hard out. Why couldn't he have gotten an easier second matchup, Olsen or Huck? He tried not to dwell in the place of that timid question. He could only move forward in spiral patterns, as was his predilection. He took a short dip in the water, and then, at noon, he danced the Elements.

His pirouettes were perfect, and his dexterity was legendary. When he arrived at the Fire Dances, he went from being a cyclone to being a flamethrower.

He moved linearly, tumbling forward and backward, throwing spinning back-kicks and knifing elbows.

From the overlook of the house on the hill, Juniper Jinn watched with a cup of coffee as Dervish danced by the lake. She saw sunfish and smallmouth bass cruising around the weeds near the shore. "Fucking spectacular," she said, moseying off.

She did her first workout of the day in the indoor gym space. She had to bind the knee and secure it in a brace. For her, toughness was a necessity. She started with clapping push-ups, four sets of twenty-five, followed by triceps extensions from a downward-facing dog pose. She did lateral raises, shoulder shrugs, pull-ups, dips, planks, side planks, side lunges, and jump squats. Ground drills and shadowboxing for thirty minutes. Finally, she swam the lake, point to point and back.

She spent a half-hour dolling herself up for an afternoon of sitting on crates near Warhole's fire and playing Bloody Knuckles with Pickup Truck Huck, whose massive bruise had migrated from his nose off to the side of his cheek and was taking on various hues. She was too quick for Huck, too unpredictable. He made a comment about sneaking off into the trees, but she ignored it.

Pickup Truck Huck continued unwarrantedly to press his point. Finally, Juniper Jinn had to sharpen her tone. "What is it about 'I'm not for you' that you don't understand? Have you ever even won a fight? Do you think prettiness is for the weak? To the weak she tends—merciful, kind, without condescension. But it is the song of the strong that this pretty life plays."

She kept studying Warhole Eleven, who didn't seem to notice her at all from behind his mirror shades.

Dmitri Petrovich was fourth to rise, in the same hour as Whirlwind Dervish and Juniper Jinn. He was first to eat: a bowl of chopped fruits steeped in whole milk, followed by a bowl of grain cereal in the same, then three eggs, two potatoes shredded and fried, six strips of smoked bacon, and a slice of sourdough bread. After breakfast, he drank shots of water out of a Karkhov bottle, a pretend Russian drinking pretend vodka.

Dmitri Petrovich wasn't Russian, couldn't put the Cyrillic alphabet in order, and he spoke with a Midwestern accent, but he did have a legendary kettlebell routine. He doubled Juniper Jinn in pure strength. His workout struck a pose balanced between the stationary power of Jinn's workout and the creative flow of Whirlwind Dervish: he did no reps but moved through various forms as if by instantaneous choice. He finished his training with bagwork on the trunk of an aspen tree, which he kicked with stout roundhouses.

Fifth up was Artemeli Skryke, who started his day at 7:00 a.m. with a walk to be with his thoughts. The sun shone in his eyes.

Physically, he was fine. A sub was, after all, just that—a sub. But the loss hurt. Not the provisional champion, not the victor, but the vanquished. It gave him an uneasy feeling—the creeping doubt, the senselessness of hope—when confronted with the fact of defeat, but do the facts mean what they say…? The arcanum of loss when addressed to a character whose nature it is to never give up. "I'll win the next one," he said aloud.

A clear statement. A call…to will unto another… in a sport whose purpose was to shed light on the facts of combat between two human individuals… what are the facts, Artemeli? "What are the facts?"

In a rematch, he gave himself a chance. But for what reason? For one, that shot was not just reckless. It was suicide. In a rematch, Artemeli's striking would show the mark of an assassin. No, he would not grapple with Heracles. He would cut him, and over the duration, he would drown him in his own blood.

PIT FC

What had given him the confidence to take that shot? What else does he know to be true that, in truth, isn't and will only be revealed to be so in the most devastating way yet?

He walked for six miles.

What if he went 0–3 and didn't make the tournament? He wanted to win in the worst way, as any bad man would. But the specter of doubt flitted around his body in strange whispers of false sensation.

It was not time to think about a rematch. There was one of six other opponents waiting for him in the Pit tonight.

He felt that Two Hawks would get the shot at the chip. So he would get Whirlwind Dervish. He felt a wave of confidence as he thought about what he would face in the blue-painted tornado man. His footsteps rode the earth.

He was the loser in Pit FC 1.
He would win Pit FC 2.

*****

Pickup Truck Huck got up at 8:30 a.m. He was pretty used to losing.

Two Hawks got up at 9:00 a.m.

He waded out to his knees in the lake, his hands darted into the water, and he lifted out a smallmouth bass. No one saw it. Juniper Jinn was out swimming. He thought Jinn was hot, and he smiled at the casual thought of jostling her.

His last girlfriend left him three months ago, and since then he had been entrenched in his training camp. Still, the fire burned hot within him—he would never admit it to Jinn. He looked the fish in the eye and let it go. He swam out and met Juniper Jinn halfway.

"I watched your fight."

"Yeh? What did you think?"

"You're a savage."

"Thanks, Two Hawks! You're about as sweet as I'm going to feel when I take that undefeated record of yours, honey. Blow me if you think I'm going to sit out here and play footsie with you."

"I'm going to go now." He swam off.

Hijinks Olsen woke up last. He had some stingers from the loss to Jinn and some bruising. He was always an oversleeper, though. He awakened groggy, a mild headache riding his mind.

He looked in the bathroom mirror, staring himself down with a look of agitated distress. He was a low, steady, ominous rumble of a man, and we shall

PIT FC

see if he had what it takes to find a win against Pickup Truck Huck. By the time he arose, the matchups had already been announced.

*****

The interviewer, with her microphone, stood between Pickup Truck Huck and Hijinks Olsen in the antechamber of the Pit.

"I ain't got a problem with you. I'll chill now and take my crack at cha later. I got three kids. I do this for them."

Olsen laughed derisively.

"Don't you share the same sentiment, Hijinks?" the interviewer said.

"I'm hardly inclined to agree with someone just because they want to get chummy with you or because they have children. You've got the cognitive capacity of a prokaryote. Though I'm inclined to think that might be to your advantage when I'm looking for a brain cell to knock out of you."

"Well, bro, I'm inclined to think that's a mighty big word for a toothless hillbilly like yourself. *Prokaryote.*"

Hijinks went silent.

"That seems to have gotten under your skin, Olsen. Do your teeth make you self-conscious?"

Hijinks stayed silent.

"C'mon, you pouter, answer the woman! She's talking to you."

Hijinks Olsen lit a death stare on Pickup Truck Huck, still holding his tongue.

"Get over here, guys. Face off."

*****

All the intensity surrounded Pit FC 2. 3.2 million viewers were in tow as Pickup Truck Huck drove across the Pit toward his opponent. He had closed a +800 DOG in the least anticipated fight of the night.

Oddsmakers had emerged overnight, with the most action surrounding the main event, featuring undefeated Dmitri Petrovich versus the undefeated Two Hawks for the provisional championship. Petrovich closed as a -200 FAV, and Two Hawks as a +165 DOG.

But here we were, with a fight in the making. Five minutes in, and it was an obvious dud. Their evasions were committal, while their attacks were not. They moved around the Pit, not hitting each other. With viewership dwindling down to 900K, the Pit FC production team sent out an option to each viewer to receive a notification when the fight had ended.

PIT FC

Ten minutes elapsed. In that time, Huck landed two leg kicks. Olsen landed once on the calf. Ten more minutes passed. Beads of sweat mottled their skin, but neither man lost a step. Ten more minutes went by.

To the audience, the fighters must have lost each other's respect. Hijinks Olsen threw a one-two jab-cross into the air, Huck evading back and to the left. Huck then stepped back to the right with the Pit wall a yard's length behind him, and as Olsen spent his attack, Huck fed him an upkick to the face that went *Fuego* on the web that night. Less than 500K viewers saw it live.

Pickup Truck Huck had a dazzled look in his upturned eyes when he spoke to the interviewer. "First-ever victory in the Pit. In any Pit. Feels great. It's sure been a long time coming. I want to thank my wife and my three kids back home. You know who you are. Daddy loves you. You've given up so much for me to be here, making history. We're gonna take a family trip to Disney World with tonight's win bonus. That's a promise."

"One I'm sure you'll be held to," the interviewer said. "Now 1–36, you finally overcame that hurdle. Did you ever believe you'd never see this day come, and now that it has, how does it feel?"

"It feels groovy. My record's not great. We both know it. But I am my own champion, and tonight I proved to all the haters that I can be a winner. A lot of people bet I'd never win even one. I hope you went broke doing it, fuckers."

"That was a really long fight, but what an amazing finish! Pickup Truck Huck, *what was that?*"

"That was the perfect game plan put into action. I sang him a lullaby, then I put the crybaby to sleep."

"You mean to tell me a thirty-five-minute standoff was the game plan?"

"Look…we both know Olsen isn't the smartest guy. I knew if I stayed in there long enough without taking too much damage, he would eventually lose his focus. When he did, I was there."

"How did you know when to pull the trigger?"

"When he kept getting lazy and staying in range, I didn't want to give away my strats early. When I finally threw that front kick, I made it count."

"You show great cardio for a guy your size."

"Thanks! I've got a great coach back home—shout-out!—and I put in my hours. The love handles are for my love back home. But don't let them fool you."

"Mind if I give one a squeeze?"

"Go ahead, honey. Grab yourself a handful of that celebrity skin."

PIT FC

"Joking!"

"Well, now you gotta gimme that squeeze. You can't lead a man on like that."

"I don't know. If you really insist—"

"Gotcha back!"

"Haha, you're a real player."

"I love my wife very much. I don't need any side squeeze."

"Well," the interviewer concluded, "that was awkward."

"You started it, Missy."

"To be fair, I did. Congratulations on a great finish and your first-ever pit-fighting win."

As he walked away, she reached out and pinched a hunk of his lower back.

The camera cut to a view from the ground above the Pit. A ramp led downward into the cavernous earth. We followed Whirlwind Dervish, his bald pate blue and glittering, as he made his descent, uttering incantations that were unintelligible to the audience.

Some believe God formed man from clay. The Pit is dug out of the same substance. Man and Pit: living flesh and carved earth, presence and absence, the conditions of one another's being, the conduits of life and struggle.

The Pit yawns, a void, a darkness from which light shines forth. The Pit always was and always will be. Its spirit has descended upon the terra, carved out through struggle and a shovel. It is the true, higher Pit that has given rise to the temporary Pit where they held Pit FC.

The Pit is scarred tissue in the face of the earth. The Pit is the place where you are who you are, and what you express is damage, given and taken. Our lives are inflictions.

The Pit knows no remorse. It does not ask to be forgiven for hurting. Instead, it asks a fighter to take on more and more pain. Toughness is the key past the threshold to the Pit.

The camera cut to Artemeli Skryke, wearing a leather jackal mask tied back with two straps, as he started down the ramp into the Pit.

The Pit knows no remorse.

Giving up less size than yesterday, in his Pit FC 1 loss to Dmitri Petrovich, Skryke was nonetheless small in stature next to 6'0" Whirlwind Dervish, with his unnaturally long arms and disproportionately short legs. In their face-off meeting with the interviewer, there was nothing but respect between the two fighters.

"It will be an honor to go to battle against you, brother."

"The honor is mine," Dervish responded.

"How easy is it for either of you to go out there and punch each other in the face when there is no animosity between you?"

"Strictly business," Dervish responded. "When the fight is over, we can hug it out."

"Have you ever been in a fight where you did not bury the hatchet afterward?"

"No. Never."

"Whirlwind Dervish, you are the more experienced fighter, at least in theory. Do you plan to outwit him? Or, what is your plan going into this fight?"

"When I close my eyes, I see myself winning by knockout."

"He can say whatever he likes, but the fact is this: in a few minutes, we're going to fight. In a fight, anything can happen."

"Artemeli Skryke, all humility aside, why do you feel you have the edge?"

"I keep saying it. I'm the Ace."

"What about you, Whirlwind?"

"I approach with the spirit of the desert. All he sees will be an illusion, a fatal mirage, and when he goes to draw breath, he will find only heat."

"Good luck, gentlemen. Face off."

They shook hands before departing into the Pit.

Artemeli Skryke began the fight by racing across the Pit and capturing Dervish by the arm as he tried to take off across the wall. He spun him around 360 degrees, using the momentum of his takeoff to throw him slamming into the Pit wall. Skryke backed off a step, and then he timed a front power kick to the sternum as Dervish came off the wall. He followed it with a straight right hand to Dervish's jaw.

Whirlwind Dervish's legs went out, and Skryke came down on top of him, raining blows. Dervish scrambled to his knees, dragging at Skryke's left arm as he took a right elbow across his cheek. The jackal looked mean, vicious, and hungry. From his base, Dervish was able to stand back up. As they broke, he rattled Skryke with a spinning backfist, followed by a looping right hand.

The jackal mask, dented, sat askew above Skryke's frame. Artemeli Skryke rolled back into a crouch.

Whirlwind Dervish, who had entered the fight as a -320 FAV, took a step back and bobbed at his knees, lifting his arms up into a traditional guard—an unusual look for the unusual Dervish. The second addition in the Whirlwind Dervish NFT collection, this clip of Dervish's bounce-back strikes and bounce-back into poise sold for $15 apiece in a limited-edition release of one thousand copies.

PIT FC

Without hesitation, Skryke dived into a low single, and elevating the leg, he forced Dervish to bounce back. With amazing dexterity, Dervish made a high attack at Skryke's head with his base leg. Skryke blocked the attack and dumped Dervish onto his butt.

Artemeli Skryke backed out of the engagement, signaling Dervish to his feet. Dervish spun low to the ground with his leg extended straight out and ascended to his feet. Skryke threw a jab-cross-uppercut combo and rotated into a spinning wheel kick, all four attacks missing narrowly.

Dervish was backed up to the wall, and he kicked off it, throwing a Superman punch. Skryke's head erupted with the absorption of the strike, but he was able to counter with a left and then a right hook. Dervish ran away, stealing across the crevice where he'd entered the Pit and picking up speed as he ran sideways across the wall.

Meeting Dervish across the Pit, Skryke cartwheeled and captured Dervish's head in his ankles as Dervish passed by. He folded forward explosively in that instant, smashing Dervish into the ground, and he climbed straight into a mounted triangle.

What appeared at first to be gurgling from Whirlwind Dervish turned out to be laughter.

Unable to finish the sub, Skryke let a scramble ensue, unlocking his legs. As he captured an arm, he stepped across the face, locking in a deep armbar. Not tapping, Dervish struggled to his feet. Rightfully, Skryke snapped the arm.

Skryke released the broken arm and spun into a hip heist to his feet. He was wet with sweat, his and Dervish's, though his leather jackal mask didn't show it. Arm broken, Whirlwind Dervish could still swing his fist like a knot of bone at the end of a rope of meat. He advanced forward, spinning, and found his mark on Skryke's face.

Skryke kicked at Dervish's knee. Dervish went southpaw, and with his left arm dangling at his side, he started to connect with the jab. He was doing it, bringing Skryke deep into the desert territory. Artemeli Skryke made a desperate-looking shot for a single, then made a second effort to a body lock. And they backed into the Pit wall. Dervish captured Skryke's head with his good arm and sat down on a guillotine, trying to lock it in with his dead hand. Ninety seconds elapsed.

Skryke's head finally popped free. He started dropping fists like a man in flames, cutting through Dervish's guard, and bashing his head into the ground again...and again...and again. Whirlwind Dervish

PIT FC

blinked in and out of consciousness, but he did not give up. An upkick connected with Skryke's jaw. He climbed to a standing position as Skryke stumbled back two steps.

Artemeli Skryke slid off to the left, dipped, and came up clean with an uppercut. At the same moment, Dervish lowered himself in symmetry with Skryke and came up clean with his own uppercut. Both opponents fell flat on their backs from the matching blows. Double knockout!

Draw.

*****

Artemeli Skryke and Whirlwind Dervish were hugging it out in the antechamber, while the interviewer showered them with praise: "A truly classic fight. No loser in this one."

Whirlwind Dervish leaned into the microphone. "The moment feels good for me and Artemeli. Much respect for him. He is a worthy opponent."

Artemeli Skryke's jackal head turned in profile next to the shoulders of Whirlwind Dervish, offering up his benediction.

Down in the antechamber, Juniper Jinn was swaying next to Warhole Eleven. She snagged the microphone from the interviewer's hands and said, "I've got the first question. What are your dimensions?"

Dramatically, he fussed about reaching over, set his hand gently on her shoulder, and, with his other hand, pried free the mic. He looked right at her, and through the reflections of his aviator shades, one can only wonder what Juniper Jinn would've seen in her image if she hadn't been staring down at Eleven's crotch. "Eleven inches of roped steel, baby."

He returned the interviewer's microphone. "Are you two prepared to *fight* in there?"

Warhole Eleven fielded this one: "I'd rather fight than fuck, but I'm good with both."

"Juniper Jinn, you seem a bit bothered. Have you ever been turned on in a fight before?"

"No."

"Is it the mustache?"

"Let's put it this way: Warhole Eleven is one big dick. He's all dick. When my babe flesh touches him, it might be all over."

"Like Juniper Jinn says, I've got big dick power, and I'm ready to push this pussy in."

"Do you have a more sensitive side?"

Jinn nodded along as he said, "I love nature, candlelit evenings, and I delight in philosophical discussion of the failures of the skeptical attitude."

PIT FC

"Is Warhole Eleven dating material? What do you think, Juniper?"

"Never date a heavyweight. That's the golden rule."

"Face off, you two."

"Two legends enter the Pit..." The interviewer went solo as Eleven and Jinn sidled through the crevice that opened into the Pit. "With an air of innuendo between them. Things are really heating up here at Pit FC 2." Her pretty face flickered in the light of two torches affixed to the opposite walls of the antechamber, whose ceiling was a little more than seven feet high. With a sheen of youth and a hint of perspiration on her brow, the interviewer wore bright red lipstick and a dress made of vertical bands of fabric, one of them peacock print and the others black and dark purple. She wore a tiara of black feathers around her neck. Her platinum hair was tied back in a ponytail with a single braid off the center. Her sensuality could not be denied. "Thank you for joining us this historic night."

As the fight went live, Warhole Eleven was a -250 FAV, and Juniper Jinn was a +225 DOG.

Warhole Eleven rapped his jaw with his knuckles, saying, "I'll give you one free crack at me, sweetie." She took it. Punched him straight in the nose.

After wiping off a trail of blood, Eleven flashed a wink at her, then came forward in a low, swooping guard. With a sharp "Ya," she threw the inside leg kick, dangerously close to the groin. She wasn't interested in talking, like she had been in the Olsen fight.

He engaged in a clinch, then stepped in, threw her over his hip, and came down in a north-south position. He rotated over into side control. He tried to slide his knee across her abdomen into the mount, but she captured the foot for a second, and he had to tug it free, grinding his elbow down into her throat. She bucked free of the suffocating pressure, and he sat up into the mount, hips bearing down into her torso. He threw a strike to the body with his left fist, then dropped into her face with the right elbow.

Warhole Eleven, with a dab of Jinn's blood darkening his forehead and another trickle of his own blood coming from his nostril, said to her, "I'll stop hurting you if you call me daddy."

"Okay, Daddy, don't hurt me." She scraped her lips across his belly hair in an awkward kiss.

He helped her up, gentlemanlike, kissed the back of her hand chivalrously, then circled away spryly from her surprise attack, making her miss with the right hand.

Eleven engaged in the clinch again. But instead of throwing an inside shot, he grabbed a handful of Jinn's breasts. Jinn squawked and grabbed him by his shorts. The live feed was cut to black, and suspicious viewers were notified of technical difficulties.

Fifteen minutes later, the feed resumed, inconclusively, with Warhole Eleven's meeting in the antechamber with the interviewer.

"That was the most fun I've ever had in a fight. A real lover's spat."

"Are you mad about how it ended?"

"I won the fight. How could I be mad?"

"The low blow afterward?"

"She owed me one for the titty-twister."

"Any hope for igniting this flame back at camp?"

"Whenever she's ready for a true heavyweight, a gentleman, and a scholar, like we all know she wants, I'll be here."

"Just so you're aware, Warhole, the second half of this fight failed to broadcast due to technical difficulties. Will you be disappointed if this victory is lost to recorded history?"

"If there's one fight I'll always carry in my heart, it's this one. If I don't have to share it with the world, all the better. Don't get me wrong, I love my fans dearly. It's just that this one…it was personal."

"Good luck making up after that beating, Warhole. Thanks for your time."

"You're a real sweetheart, Miss Interviewer. The world doesn't deserve you."

She blushed, glancing directly into the camera lens. She belonged to the audience now, and they loved her. The next cut went to a shot above the Pit, showing two silhouetted figures hovering at the edge while oak trees and aspen lurked darkly all around them. The camera looked up at a barn owl perched on a branch, looking down as if from an endless distance.

*****

The Pit subdues vagrant dreams, dismantles idle chatter, and cuts down the hero in his hubris. The Pit is a circle, but not a wheel. The outcomes are permanent, immutable, fixed in time, and recorded. Tonight, one undefeated fighter would lose that prestige. The Pit is risk and opportunity—for a person to elevate himself over another who wants the same thing you want.

The Pit is a measure of man's vitality. It is an unwavering tableau of the vision of the fighter. It is all love.

Pit fighters respect each other because they do what others don't and know what others can't. It is all just a trick of perception that makes the Pit a value of entertainment. Its true value is its veracity. Nothing about it can be discussed or disputed except that which is already in excess.

But it is not like an apple core discarded—this obscured and effaced truth. It is like an eagle descended, and its feast is all its own.

Vagrant dreams become nightmares in the Pit. One can assume that one of these two fighters, being the who and the what that they are, will not be sleeping well tonight. Pit FC 2 ascends to new pinnacles of greatness. This stands to be the fight of a lifetime for all of us.

*****

After the entrancing nature imagery had given way to a long shot of the antechamber, framing Two Hawks and provisional champion Dmitri Petrovich in the interviewer's ken of dancing firelight, there was no more daylight left. The twilight feeling buzzed about the three standing before us.

The interviewer, now in close-up, set the stage: "The main event looms large as two undefeated fighters prepare to put their unmarred records on the line for the Pit FC provisional championship and for glory unknown to common days. This is a statement fight, and we can all agree that the winner of this fight tonight should be favored to win it all.

"Could the unnatural onslaught of Two Hawks efface the transcendent pride of Dmitri Petrovich? Answers seek their causes in the events that follow."

The viewership had swollen past four million for the first time in Pit FC history.

The interviewer, diminutive next to Dmitri Petrovich, asked him what the source of his confidence was.

"I am a ruthless fighter. I have speed, strength, and stamina. I have skills. I have cunning. And I don't think any man on earth can stop me."

"What is your plan of attack?"

"First I crush his will, then I crush his body."

"Two Hawks," the interviewer said, turning to the 5'11" man with the black, white, and red face paint, "How do you feel right now, standing next to the crusher, Dmitri Petrovich?"

"I feel great. I want only the best fights, and Petrovich is that. I want my valor to be witnessed. In the Pit, the whole world stops and watches. Outside the Pit, God is your only witness. I want to shake the foundations of the world with my fights. When you watch, I want you to forget yourself so completely that maybe, just maybe, the world inside you dies."

PIT FC

"And in its place?"

"The vessel fills with holy light."

"Dmitri Petrovich, Two Hawks, this fight is for the provisional championship of Pit FC. The winner will continue to tomorrow's main event.

"Square off."

Two Hawks stood straight as a rail, looking up into the ghoulish holographic eyes of Petrovich's plastic skull mask, his fists covering his chin. "I'm sorry for your loss."

"Go to the mountains, where only the strong make their way," Petrovich said. "Pit FC is my mountain!"

The interviewer stood alone, the glitter from Whirlwind Dervish's makeup shimmering in the black feathers of her tiara, the two combatants slipping into the Pit behind her, vanishing like spectral images into the nothingness beyond. "To our viewing audience, we thank you from the bottom of our hearts. We're as excited to be here as we hope you are. We love all the interaction. Stay with us, world. We know you're watching. Provisional champion Dmitri Petrovich versus Two Hawks is live."

*****

A huge hole in Petrovich's mask had opened beneath his right eye, and on the bare skin a welt was visible. Two Hawks already had him tiring. He would step out of range, come back in, angle out again, and step in again at the same time as Petrovich, but just beat him to the target.

Dmitri Petrovich was chasing him all over, his wind picking up, and he wasn't landing at all. He had taken four right hands to the same spot. He was stinging, frustrated, and getting angry. He bull-rushed Two Hawks, stuffing the knee Hawks threw as Petrovich closed, and pressed him back against the Pit wall. Petrovich came over with a thudding right elbow to the dome. Two Hawks's palms hit the ground, then he rolled forward and dashed away.

In another impossible move that was forever immortalized by the Pit FC production crew, Two Hawks ran straight up the Pit wall, sprung backward off the top, flipping through the night sky with one full rotation, and came down with a flying kick across Petrovich's face. Dmitri Petrovich went out.

Knockout of the Year!

Two Hawks sat down with Dmitri Petrovich, taking his head into his lap as he called him back to consciousness. He softly spoke soothing words to the fallen champion, whose message the audience could only speculate on.

"Did you practice that?"

"In my dreams."

"What was your plan going into the fight?"

Before Two Hawks could respond, Dmitri Petrovich stormed up to them and stole the microphone. "I want a rematch. You're a coward that relies on cheap tricks. But," he said, pointing a finger and thumb at Two Hawks, "you can't fool me twice."

Petrovich lumbered off.

"Anything else for us?"

"If he earns the rematch, we'll do it again. Until then, give me Warhole Eleven. I'll pit my two KOs against his."

"We can't wait. Go enjoy your championship. Still undefeated."

Pit FC 3

They all shared the same dream. They did not have to like each other. When they awoke, in turn, the morning of Pit FC 3, they did have to live together.

Artemeli Skryke and Two Hawks rummaged out a pair of fishing rods from the unfinished basement. They stalked the croaking frogs down by the shoreline, filling up a wicker basket with the hopping creatures. They hooked the frogs for bait. From the shore, they cast their lines. They waited.

Both bobbers dipped simultaneously, and their reels strained audibly as the slack pulled from either line before they set their hooks, one after another. The joy of fishing is the joy of the fight. They each fought their fish to the earth, lifting them on land with a net. They were two Northern pikes, which Two Hawks filleted and fried for lunch. "Two fish for us," Two Hawks said.

"Thank you, bro." Artemeli Skryke flashed a charming smile the audience would never see.

*****

Hijinks Olsen woke early this morning, at 7:15 a.m., with twice the headache he'd awakened to yesterday. He took a green kayak out on the still lake. There was dew on the grass he crossed barefoot to the lake to set the craft to water.

As he paddled around the perimeter, he encountered a showdown between two loons, their flock circling agitatedly around the animated birds. The two males rose up out of the water, wings outspread, shrieking at each other. One loon backed down, made the gesture of swimming away, then darted back to rejoin the circle.

This electrifying display captured Hijinks Olsen's imagination. He envisioned encoded in every fight the tension between one man's dominance and another's defiance. He would never express this insight to anyone.

*****

After fishing, Artemeli took to the hills and the country roads for another walk.

Double knockout!

He felt, if anything, more dismal than yesterday. It was the fight of the night, yes, but he had been beaten in his own game. What was next for him? "Yes, what's next?"

It was between Olsen and Huck. Would he get the winner or the loser? They were both, in his mind, losers. Weak men. Not of the caliber of his last two opponents. There was no doubt in his mind that he would choke either one. "Cinch it in, bro."

He thought, as he walked, of Hijinks Olsen and of Pickup Truck Huck as the same opponent, the losing denominator between them. He would win in commanding fashion, and they would have to let him into the tournament. They would have to show respect for his name. "Cinch it in, bro."

Five miles went by.

*****

Two Hawks left the filets to cool in the fridge. He stripped down to his boxer briefs. He swam out and met Juniper Jinn halfway across the lake again.

"Hey there, lover boy."

PIT FC

"Juniper—"

"Yesterday, you could've taken me. Warhole Eleven is my man now," she interrupted him, "and I am his."

Two Hawks dipped down beneath the surface, then kicked his way back up. He blinked water out of his eyes, which he fixed like twin blades on Juniper Jinn. "I'm going to knock him out."

"I hope you do, kid. Avenge my loss. It's not going to change anything."

He slipped down under the water again, her frame hovering around the stud of her belly button in the haze of the water before him. She slipped under after him. They shared that moment, looking blurrily into one another's eyes.

Two Hawks dipped down farther into the water, swimming off with frog kicks. Juniper Jinn pulled at the water, trying to follow him, but he disappeared into the darkness, and she had to come up for air.

*****

In the afternoon, Juniper Jinn took out her tarot cards to play a three-way game of war with Pickup Truck Huck and Two Hawks. Warhole Eleven tended his fire, chomped apples, read the Bible, and made eyes with Juniper Jinn. Without shades, he was a blue-eyed, black-haired man, peeking into her soul. Jinn scored the game, acting as the moderator of its peculiar machinations.

Huck played the Ten of Swords. Everyone had to discard one. Jinn played the Page of Cups. Two Hawks played Temperance.

"Temperance wins." Two Hawks collected the trick.

He led with the Six of Wands. Jinn played the Six of Pentacles, declared no trump, and played her second card, the Four of Cups. Huck played the Ten of Wands. Everyone passed a card to their right. "Draw. Sudden death."

Jinn was down to one card: Strength. Huck countered with Death. "We need clarification."

She cut the deck. "The Moon."

She explained, "Although love is stronger than death, the sun is to life as the moon is to death. Death wins."

Huck took the loaded trick.

Jinn drew three cards to a full hand; Two Hawks and Pickup Truck both drew two.

Huck led with the Magician. Jinn sluffed the Ace of Cups. Two Hawks played the Fool. "Everyone, discard your hand, draw five cards, and lay one at random."

Jinn turned the King of Swords, Huck the Nine of Swords, and Two Hawks the Eight of Pentacles. Jinn scooped up the bonus trick.

"Now, discard your hand and draw three. Then the first person to flip a three or the Empress wins. On his third flip, Two Hawks turned the Three of Cups and took the stacked trick.

Seven cards for Huck and Hawks, three for Jinn.

Last, Two Hawks led the Wheel of Fortune. Huck followed with Judgment. Jinn played the Hanged Man and was out. "One cut for the whole game."

The World.

"Is the World the stage of the ups and downs of fortune? Or does judgment dictate the world, judging us even as we are also the ones who judge? We need one last clarification. Hopefully nothing from the minor arcana."

"What is it?" Two Hawks asked.

The Hermit.

"Two Hawks wins. Take a cut for your free fortune."

"Yay," he said, cutting the cards.

"Why did he win?!"

"The Hermit looks within, while Judgment looks without. Man, as he turns inward on the path of the Hermit, sees in his relationship with the World all the turns and vicissitudes of the Wheel.

"Oh, honey," Jinn said, seeing Two Hawks's cut for the first time.

"The Lovers."

Two Hawks noticed Warhole Eleven in this instance, watching them with apparent disinterest.

"I didn't mean to pull you like this."

"Is that an apology?"

Jinn winced, whether at his question or the twisted knot at the pit of her core, wondering whether what she wanted was what she wanted.

"Be careful, Warhole. He knows things I cannot even discern."

"I'm not losing to that twerp. I don't care if he sold his soul to beat me. I'm not losing."

"You're a man of the way, the truth, and the life."

"Yes, Miss, I am."

"Two Hawks is like an ancient child, cavorting beneath the firmament. He trespasses through portals to powers unseen. I fear for your life if you were to threaten what he wants."

Warhole bit deep into an apple and spat seeds. "I'm not afraid to die."

"What about me? Am I between you and what you want, love?"

PIT FC

"No."

Hijinks Olsen, taken to wander the peripheries of other people's scenes, watched dementedly as they kissed, their lips opening and closing on one another. He watched as someone might watch a scene of horror unfold, waiting for the awful turn from bad to worse. Warhole caught Hijinks staring, and he stared right back, pulling Jinn in by the waist and squeezing her.

The lovers retreated to Warhole's cot.

*****

Juniper Jinn splashed the mic with her bright energy. "I wore pigtails for Pickup Truck Huck. He's perverted like that."

"Looking good nonetheless."

"*You're* looking good, girl!"

The interviewer was wearing a purple blouse with silver lines and a platinum skirt to match her hair, cut just above the shoulder. The top buttons of her blouse were undone. The cut of her skirt was halfway up her thigh. She had pink lipstick and green makeup around her eyes.

"You're a vixen."

"That means a lot coming from the legend herself."

"Aren't we the prettiest pair you'd ever see in a Pit?"

"You seem to be in high spirits today, almost bubbly. What are your emotions, if any, going into this fight?"

"Let me tell you a secret, love. Promise not to tell anyone."

"If you tell me, the whole world will know."

"The whole world doesn't know shit…If I know the guy I'm fighting fights with a lot of passion and heat, I'll toy up my clit real nice in the moments before the fight. Get all those pheromones floating around. I can send him into a tizzy before the fight even starts. But we all know Pickup Truck Huck isn't that guy."

*****

"Thank you for giving me the stage and for asking all sorts of great questions. You make us fighters accessible to our fans. That's why this event is such a success. People can kind of relate to us."

"You're welcome, Pickup Truck. I love the job."

"And I love your outfit. Very sexy."

"Don't worry. I know you love your wife very much."

"See, my old lady swears she doesn't mind if I have a side squeeze, as long as I'm winning fights.

PIT FC

Now that I have won one, I could be in the looking. And you're looking fine in that skirt, Miss Lady."

"You're an endlessly positive guy, Pickup Truck. So don't make me slap you. Just tell me, how have you stayed so happy and upbeat through all the defeats?"

"It's the endorphins, the getting punched silly day in and day out. And just knowing, win or lose, I'm living my best life out here for my kids back home."

"Would you like to respond to Juniper Jinn calling you a pervert?"

"What was that?"

"Oh, nothing. You're a greasy cad. But I'll still wish you luck in there. Don't get beaten up by a girl."

*****

Juniper Jinn opened the fight with a kick to the groin. She followed it with a knee to the groin of her stooped opponent.

Pickup Truck Huck went down into the fetal position. Juniper Jinn closed to finish the fight. L3B, the owner of Pit FC, rushed the Pit, looking to restrain Juniper Jinn.

Jinn looked up. L3B slapped her. She grabbed him by the junk. He grabbed her by the hair—showdown. Big Bam Bam, L3B's brother, slid down the twelve-foot wall into the Pit, charged Juniper Jinn, grabbed her by the jaw, and lifted her into the air. Bam Bam held her face up to his and said, "We want a fair fight."

Jinn bunched her lips as if to respond, but she couldn't.

"Blink once if you agree."

Dutifully, she blinked.

Big Bam Bam set her down. The fight resumed.

Juniper Jinn hit Huck with the same two low blows, the upkick and the knee. He collapsed to the ground, grabbing his groin and howling madly.

Right away, L3B and Big Bam Bam showed up again. Jinn threw dirt in L3B's face, then hit him with a double-eye poke. She went deep into horse stance, down to the level of L3B, who was on his knees, clutching his eyes in his hands and moaning eerily, and she came up with a headbutt into Big Bam Bam's crotch. He sat down, bellowing. Then Jinn turned and kneed the kneeling L3B in the balls. He fell sideways into the bottom of his own Pit.

All three men were down, groaning, or worse. Juniper Jinn arched her back, then spat.

"Do you feel a sense of resolution with that matchup?"

"I beat ass against three grown men. If that ain't resolution, I don't know what is."

"How do you feel about your reputation as a dirty fighter?"

"Men always say they are the stronger sex. Simply false. If I can get to his balls, I can bring down any man. It's as simple and as pathetic as that."

She left her with a fist bump. "Huck deserved it," the interviewer said.

*****

There are cries in the night. If one didn't know better, one might think of them as the cries of the unadulterated intensities that arise when two bodies go to war against one another in the Pit. If the Pit were Hell, then why do so many pine for it so irrationally, from the seat of their wills? And what does one long for in it? To show out, to test one's mettle, to see what one is made of. It is proof of the quality of life, extracted from a quantity of days. Without the Pit, everything would melt into nothingness.

Look into your heart. Do you have what it takes? The desire to do and to know? This desire is born of Pit. Or do you languish in the haze of an incorporeal awareness? In other words, do you say "no" only, and for that which calls you, there is no "yes?"

BRENDEN HAUKOS

If the interviewer looks into her heart, standing there next to Artemeli Skryke, she will see that it is beaming. To Skryke, the look in her eyes says only "yes."

The Spirit of Conflict imbues the Pit with its glimmering menace. Some are called; most are not.

The Pit is an icon. It stands as a monument to all struggle in the effort of every "yes." God spoke the Pit into being. It is a miracle, as are all things.

You could wander for years, looking for the Pit. If it doesn't call you, you will never find it. One steps into the Pit for oneself alone. The rest is the lie that must be told. The interviewer is here to administer the lie.

But why must the lie be told? What makes it necessary? It is told to answer the lies within ourselves as those lies reach outward. In the Pit, all lies go mute. This is what makes it so mesmerizing.

The Pit is a miracle, as are all things.

*****

The interviewer looked mesmerized by the presence of Artemeli Skryke. "I'm here with my man, Artemeli."

He pulled her close, wrapping her in his arm for the duration of the interview. With one hand, she maneuvered the microphone, and with the other,

PIT FC

she entertained Skryke's abdomen. "I hope I'm not a distraction."

"You're perfect!" She flinched in his embrace.

"Do you feel fear before a fight?"

"I haven't seen enough from Hijinks Olsen to fear him. I don't think he poses a real threat."

*****

Hijinks Olsen said, "I've got nothing to say to anybody." And that was all he had to say.

"I'd be surprised," she baited him, but he just stared at her, his right eye tracking crossways, and she finished, "if you didn't lose again."

"This is Pit FC 3," she said, while he walked away, glaring back over his shoulder at her until he disappeared into the Pit. "This is our second fight tonight. Both of these fighters look for their first Pit FC victory. This could be an elimination match for the tournament tomorrow at Pit FC 4: A Night to Crown a Champion. Be sure to join us for the finale. But for now, let's go inside the Pit where today's event is happening."

In this, his third fight, Hijinks Olsen went down like the sun, like it was inevitable. Artemeli Skryke had him backing on his heels. When he shot and captured the left leg, Olsen hopped back on one foot to the Pit wall. Skryke pulled the leg and, circling away, dragged Olsen onto his ass.

Skryke passed the legs into side control. Olsen scissored his legs and turned over toward his knees, trying to frame on Skryke, while Skryke punched him in the head. Olsen gave up his back, and Skryke pounced on it.

He locked Olsen in a body triangle and, after hand fighting, cinched in the rear naked choke. Tonight Skryke wore a dun green leather mask the shape of a snapping turtle, and the gnarly pointed mouth hovered menacingly next to Olsen's ear, looking ready to bite.

With both hands fighting the choke, Olsen labored to his feet. He bent at the knees and launched himself backward, trying to dislodge Skryke's grip with a slam. Skryke hunched forward, as if to whisper turtle thoughts. He held the choke. After a few seconds, Olsen frantically tapped.

The interviewer wouldn't get so lovey-dovey with Skryke in his post-fight interview. She may've been reprimanded on the side, chastised for her informal behavior. She questioned him: "You showed real urgency going into this fight. How did you keep your nerves in check and stay in the moment?"

"I always have the utmost confidence in myself and my skill set. I know I'm the real guy to beat on

PIT FC

the Pit FC roster. There's no one here who could beat me twice."

"I love the confidence, Artemeli."

The editing crew smudged his appearance with a blurry face. He had removed his mask. "Got to keep the player haters guessing."

"What is your level of confidence in making the tournament tomorrow?"

"Very. I've got a lot of reasons to be optimistic."

"Care to share your prediction for tonight's main event?"

"Warhole Eleven and Two Hawks?"

"Yes."

"I think Warhole Eleven has the size, and he knows how to use his body. I don't think Two Hawks has ever fought anyone quite like him, big and slick."

"What about his knockout of Dmitri Petrovich last night? Were you impressed by that?"

"To be honest, I think he got lucky. Nothing but respect to both men, but Dmitri got lucky against me, and Two Hawks got lucky against him. My dollar says Warhole knocks him out. Goodnight."

"Congratulations on a dominant performance." Then, in hushed tones, "Proud of you."

*****

Whirlwind Dervish had his left arm in a sling, but he was going to fight on. Toughness was not a doubt in his mind.

"How do you plan to fight through this?"

"It is nothing. I do not give up."

"No easy fights for you, Whirlwind. How do you approach the stout challenge of Dmitri Petrovich?"

"I shall be as breath, approaching, then receding. In the decisive moment, I shall from nowhere and from nothing strike."

"How does Whirlwind Dervish define the martial arts?"

"It is the way…the way of defending what is precious in the face of all that is base and defiled. A fight…that is a fun thing, but also just a fight. In martial arts, this is what matters: it is called love."

"No one can doubt your courage. Or your love for the fight. You're a brave warrior. Good luck out there."

*****

Dmitri Petrovich, behind his fractured skull mask, looked like he was looking down the interviewer's shirt. "You're coming off your first loss. What has changed since last night?"

"Nothing's changed. Nothing."

"What are your thoughts going into this one?"

"Thoughts? What thoughts? I am action and only action."

"You said your mother was a philosopher."

"My father."

"Your father was a philosopher. Then you said you made philosophy with your fist. If you had to make philosophy with your mind, what would your deepest thought be?"

"Do what you must do. That is all. It's as simple and as potent as that."

"I must send you in there. Good luck, Dmitri."

*****

Whirlwind Dervish started the fight on the offensive. He opened with a three-kick combination of strikes to the leg, the side, and the head; he then turned his hip over and threw an axe kick with the opposite leg. Petrovich's mask crackled and spilled shards of white plastic. A slow trickle of blood dripped from his chin.

Unfazed, Dmitri Petrovich ripped the body, punching through Dervish's bound arm. Dervish hunched over, perchance lanced through the arm with pain, perchance the wind knocked out of him. Or perchance it was a lure, as Dervish snaked his good arm around Petrovich's neck, and he used it to throw up a flying triangle.

Stuck in Dervish's knobby legs, Petrovich held Whirlwind Dervish by his back, took two tiny steps forward, and then drove Dervish down into the ground with all his brutish strength. The production crew registered the sounds of Dmitri Petrovich's neck popping and crackling as it ripped free of Dervish's legs.

Stunned, zinging, and breathless, Dervish could not resist when Dmitri Petrovich smothered him. Petrovich finished the fight, ripping Dervish's good arm with a brutal kimura.

"You've been said to have the best kimura in the game. Anything more to say on that?"

"I've got the best game in the game."

"Did you try to break his shoulder?"

"I did break his shoulder."

"Were you born mean, or did life make you this way?"

"I came out of my mama sideways."

"Ouch. Who do you predict to win the main event?"

"Doesn't matter—fake championship. I'm the real champion. We'll see you tomorrow, beautiful lady. But let me ask you a question: will you wear green tomorrow for Dmitri Petrovich?"

"Is that your favorite color?"

"So to speak."

"I'll wear my emerald dress. But it should be no secret who has my support."

"The wimp. Artemeli Skryke. Who I broke in two. It's no secret that women go for wimps these days."

"There's someone out here for everyone."

"I am not worried by these…distractions. My life is to fight. I just know you will be stunning in green for my fans at home. Thank you to those who stuck with me through the loss. I'm not going anywhere."

"I hope you can enjoy your win."

"I do."

*****

"Another night has arisen, and the main event is upon us. Undefeated provisional champion Two Hawks defends his title against Warhole Eleven, another legend of the sport."

Warhole Eleven chuckled. "Good evening, interviewer. Good to see you again."

"What do you find so amusing?"

"My last prefight meeting opened with Juniper Jinn asking for my dimensions."

"You don't have to remind me, good sir."

"I should know better."

"You should know better than to think I'd ask the same question twice."

"Got it!"

"Eleven inches of roped steel, baby!"

"Baby!"

"This is a feel-good moment for your fan base. You earned the last shot at a provisional title—you earned it the hard way."

"This feels amazing. I do feel that I've earned every cubic inch of this opportunity. Most of my fans certainly don't see past their own reflections when it comes to me, but I love them anyway. I'm not, in the end, a representative of the bizarre or of skeptical nihilism, as some seem to think. I fight for the way, the truth, and the life. Doubt cuts the way short…a bitter end. I didn't come this far by casting doubt on myself, my path, or the way of my Lord and Savior."

"How do you reconcile your staunch faith with the layer of obscenity with which you cloak yourself?"

"This is a mean business. Don't pretend it's not. Purity can't last without armor."

PIT FC

"Warhole Eleven, armored in obscenity, steps into the Pit to stake his claim on the coveted provisional championship. He's ready for Pit FC 3, and whether we believe him, whether we believe his faith is sincere, or not…all of this to say, whether or not we assume he is a good man, we cannot doubt that he is, in fact, a man. It takes balls to step into the Pit and await your opponent.

"Especially when that opponent is 15–0 pit-fighting sensation Two Hawks, who is joining us now. Another big moment for you tonight, with the opportunity to defend your championship and secure your spot in the grand finale tomorrow. How have you been coping with the pressure?"

"I always do me, and I can't be trusted to do anything else. I always trust a pure winner lives inside of me, and he will come out when I need him."

"It almost sounds like a dissociative state. Do you have trouble identifying with the person you are in the Pit?"

"Not at all. He is the real Two Hawks, the indomitable fighter, the frenzied berserker, the trampler of hopes and dreams. This is who I am, and everything that comes in between is…it's like a mirage that tries to snare your attention away from your true spiritual aims. I can only express gratitude to L3B and the Pit

FC team for giving me the space to be myself for a brief moment."

"Is it a bittersweet feeling, reflecting on your career and work?"

"My work is in making my dreams a reality. This is not bittersweet."

"Some may call the state you enter into in your fights a form of ecstasy. Do you connect with a higher power in your fights?"

"Let me tell you something. I come from a place where time folds over onto itself with deafening, rending sounds, peals, and roars, where the sundered layers of our unfolding lives melt into one another, and the coagulating substance of our lives bubbles with the breath of spirit as it churns as if in a cauldron. This is the violence that permeates all creation, and I am its servant, vanquishing all who would stand alone against two hawks, the nightmare birds of my sacred dreamscapes."

"Your words always take us to such unreal places. The insight is really appreciated. Now, go fight."

"I shall."

*****

PIT FC

A couple of minutes into the fight, Two Hawks's strategy was clear. He was attacking the body. He jabbed the liver and ripped the lower abdomen. But it appeared Warhole Eleven was too tough, too resilient, to be enervated by these petty stabs. Two Hawks was getting ahead on points, but there were no points in pit fighting, so it was no matter.

Warhole Eleven threw a spinning wheel kick that looked more like a flying V and that chopped Two Hawks across the face and to the ground. Major swelling formed above Two Hawks's left eye, disfiguring his darkly handsome features. His pupils went completely black. He rose from the ground like a stampede and rushed Warhole Eleven, lifting him up into his arms, carrying him in explosive steps up the Pit's wall, and setting him perched precipitously on the edge of the wall, so that he fell back down a moment after Two Hawks scrambled down.

Warhole Eleven landed gracefully as a cat and started toward Two Hawks in a conventional stance. For a minute, it turned into a boxing match. Two Hawks deflected Eleven's heavier blows, but his rips to the body were of no avail. Warhole Eleven, though unhurt, showed patches of red across his pale midriff.

Eleven landed a powerful hook to the side of the head. Two Hawks's ear was partially dislocated from his skull. Two Hawks ignored the ear and started kicking Eleven's lead calf, again to no avail. Warhole Eleven ate the calf kicks and cracked him with a straight right hand. The sutures above Hawks's right eye split apart, and his face became a monstrosity of disproportion on one side and of gashes and gushing blood on the other side.

Two Hawks tried to connect with leaping elbows to Eleven's head, but he couldn't find him, and all the while he was getting pieced up. He got tagged with a jab, took a blow to the torso, went down to one knee, stood back up, took a straight to the front of the chin, and went down straight and hard onto one knee.

Warhole Eleven hovered over him, seeking a finish. Two Hawks dived upside-down onto Warhole Eleven's left leg, snaked his leg up Eleven's leg, drove his other heel hard into Eleven's opposite hip, off-balancing him, then swam over while pulling Eleven's inside arm down so that Eleven tipped forward. Two Hawks swung his hip and leg around, capturing the other shoulder with the omoplata for the quick tap. Submission victory!

Two Hawks, battered up, declined the post-fight interview. Warhole Eleven commented in his stead: "It was a brilliant sub. One of the very best. Bravo, Two Hawks. I'll get you in the rematch."

Pit FC 4

"Come! Let us laugh together now, for all the pain in the world is as nothing to those of us who wander this hearty continent!" Two Hawks regaled them between his first and second puffs before he passed the joint to Warhole.

The night before Pit FC 4, a bag of marijuana materialized in Two Hawks's possession. The weed was dusty and dry. They determined Warhole Eleven had the best available paper for a joint wrap in his Bible. Eleven insisted they use a page from his favorite book, Matthew. Two Hawks rolled two joints from a page of Chapter Thirteen.

For Dmitri Petrovich, cannabis was a hard no.

The smoke put Hijinks Olsen into a stupor. While everyone else laughed and carried on, he stared at the space around his feet.

Warhole Eleven stocked up the fire, then tried to sneak off with Juniper Jinn to skinny-dip. Pickup

Truck Huck saw them leave and tagged along. "I don't want to see your dick, you jerk."

"Then don't look." He waded into his knees and stood there like a prehistoric man, shining in the moonlight.

"Fuck you, Huck."

"You're gonna wish you did."

"I'm gonna tell your wife."

"Don't have one. For real. Or any kids."

"Isn't that ripe? Answer's still no. I'm taken."

Warhole had swum off and was treading water a way out. She dived across the surface of the water and came up next to him. As she lingered over him, their bodies touched in random places.

"Blow me in the water, baby," she exclaimed. "It's my fantasy!"

Pickup Truck Huck stood there with his Candy Ass sagging above gentle waves, while Jinn's grunts, giggles, and groans traveled across the lake. She howled when she came, laughing riotously afterward and digging her nails into Warhole's chest. It all felt so good. Pickup Truck Huck's buzz, however, was killed.

*****

PIT FC

The interviewer stood out in full daylight in the center of the Pit. The show had begun. Dressed for the finale, she wore her shiny emerald dress, her hair tied back in two conjoining braids, powder-white in the face accentuating her blue lipstick, and heavy mascara.

As awkward as she may have been in some ways, her looks could kill. The audience showed love for the interviewer. Maestro_88 wrote: "Shout-out to the interviewer, our anonymous darling. Her questions have been spot-on. The in-depth look into these fighters' minds has added a special dimension to this grand spectacle. Long live Pit FC!"

She was on the microphone. "Welcome to all our live viewers." There were five and a half million to start. "Thanks for joining us for Pit FC 4: A Night to Crown a Champion. Four finalists will contend in our tournament bracket for a chance to face provisional champion Two Hawks for the prestigious title of Grand Champion and the prize bonus of $100,000."

"In mere moments, we are going to meet with all five of tonight's combatants. But first, I have a very special guest. Here's the man who started it all: the founder and owner of Pit FC, L3B!"

The camera panned to show the man behind the scenes, stocky of build, dressed vulgarly in a black-and-white striped shirt and a bandit's bandana. Through the eye-slits in the black bandana, his eyes appeared to be puffy and red.

"What inspired Pit FC?"

"I've been a lifelong student of the martial arts—it is my first love—and an avid fan of pit fighting for just as long. I grew up watching legends like Harrison Juxely and Arbrod Kilton, to name a couple early favorites. This was back when you had to watch on VHS tape and cut copies for your friends.

"Anyway, I saw an opportunity to make a mark in the history of the sport, and I ran with it. Props to my big brother for digging the Pit. Without him, none of this is possible."

"L3B, for the record, what does your name stand for?"

"My big brother is Big Bam Bam. I am Less Big Bam Bam, or L3B for short."

"Mystery solved. Thank you for enlightening us. What do you love most about pit fighting?"

"How to describe it? It's a special feeling you get when you watch a fight and think, 'This is a really good fight,' you know? It's the back-and-forth. It's the heart of a champion on full display. It's all the marbles on the line. Something for the moment. Something for the ages."

"Let's talk about the events we've already had. What was your favorite fight from Pit FC 1?"

"Two Hawks versus Whirlwind Dervish. When Dervish cut him with the elbow…such a big moment. And for Two Hawks to come back the way he did, hurt like that…unbelievable."

"What about Pit FC 2?"

"I want to say Pickup Truck Huck with his first pit victory. I believed in the guy when no one else did, and I gave him a chance where no one else would. He didn't make the tourney, but with that knockout, he at least proved himself to be a real fighter."

"You want to say Huck versus Olsen, but—"

"But who can forget the double knockout?"

"Skryke versus Dervish…"

"To say nothing is Two Hawks's KO of the century in the main event. Every night has been special, but just how special was Pit FC 2?"

"Which brings us to the question everyone's asking. When do we get to see the lost footage of Warhole Eleven versus Juniper Jinn?"

"There is no footage. It was lost."

"A lot of suspicion surrounding what happened while the cameras were off."

"That's just people. They'll always be that way."

"Let's talk about Pit FC 3."

"Let's not."

"A rough day at the office yesterday for the Bam Bam brothers. Any thoughts of disqualifying Juniper Jinn?"

"No, but she's out anyway."

"Juniper's out? Is she injured?"

"I'll let her tell you herself what's up. All I can tell you is that she won't fight. Dmitri Petrovich is getting the first-round bye."

"Artemeli Skryke and Warhole Eleven in round one?"

"An intriguing matchup."

"I would think so. But why didn't you choose a replacement for Jinn?"

"Who do we have to replace her? Dervish? Huck? Olsen? With one win between the three, and Dervish, who looked the best of all of them, with two broken arms. No, we're not diluting anything tonight."

He took a beat, then went on, "Also, I want to take this opportunity to thank you, dear interviewer. Sorry, I can't call you by name. But I will be rewarding you with a $10,000 bonus to your contract. You've been a great addition to the team and an

PIT FC

invaluable piece of the final product. The questions and comments were yours alone. I can honestly say, one or two awkward moments aside, you were brilliant. I only hope we can bring you back if we ever do this again."

"I would never miss it," the interviewer said, tearing up a little bit. "Thank you so much, and for your kind words too."

"You deserve it all."

"Thank you. But before I let you go, I would be remiss if I didn't ask you if you favored anyone to win tonight."

"As boss, I don't play favorites. Any one of those four would make a great champion for Pit FC."

"Any words you'd like to leave the audience with? Any questions I did not ask?"

"I won't make a single penny in this whole affair. Production, recruitment, prize money—it's all out of pocket. And everything we're doing online is totally anonymous. As an unsanctioned and utterly unlawful enterprise, Pit FC will go down as both a major public success and a total fiscal loss, for the protection of everyone involved. The world will never be ready for Pit FC.

"This is my legacy. Come dawn, I shall stand in total victory. To everyone who tuned in tonight, I love you all. These memories we share will never be lost. This was all for you, and I give it to you freely. You're welcome!"

*****

L3B is a prophet of the Pit. He breathes life into its inert form. Without breath, the Pit sleeps. Its dreams touch so many lives, so many who say "no" and the few who say "yes." It sleeps beneath the soil. Those who find it dirty their hands when seeking.

Hollow lives capsize in the waters of their own intricacy. The strength of the fighter is his simplicity. His life is straightforward: hard work and training, replenishment, and rest. All in preparation for and anticipation of that one moment in time, that one moment in the Pit, to make a play for glory, the ultimate resplendence.

The Pit is a mark made by man. It is a celebration of the fighting spirit—that spirit that goes down fighting, in the end, for the love of it. Love is the silent whisper beckoning in the obscurity of your mind.

Go in simplicity to that which calls you. We know these four did.

*****

PIT FC

Artemeli Skryke, Warhole Eleven, Dmitri Petrovich, and Two Hawks. They stood in an informal line, two on each side of the interviewer. All were radiating their specific signatures of being.

"The first question is for Two Hawks. One fight for the whole nugget. Just how confident are you in getting it done tonight and taking home the championship?"

"Very confident."

"Who of these three do you see as your greatest threat?"

"The only threat is within."

"Do you feel any of the damage going into tonight?"

"Nothing that will hinder my abilities."

"Thank you, Two Hawks. What about you, Warhole Eleven? Are you feeling any nicks or bruises?"

"Nothing that I'm going to complain about. Listen! All glory to God. For those of you who see us up on this stage, hidden behind the paint and the masks, and think this is a gag, it's not. I can laugh about this or that…my sexuality, for one…and I just could be in love, too…but listen, this is serious. Nothing comes before God. To have a personal relationship with Jesus Christ, your Lord and Savior, is what life is all about.

"I am so thankful God has given me this opportunity today to step into the Pit and fight for what may be the greatest distinction our sport has ever known. I am so thankful for all my fans. I love you all. Remember: Strait is the gate, narrow is the way, and few are those who find it."

"Thank you for your message, Warhole. You were obviously speaking from the heart. There are a lot of people out—"

"Give me this," Dmitri Petrovich said, yanking the microphone away from the interviewer. "These two are buffoons. Why bother listening to them? And him, scrawny boy, I already broke him in two. Two Hawks, listen carefully…" At this, Two Hawks squared off with Petrovich, raising his right eyebrow, and Petrovich went on, "Tonight I'm going to expose you to the world. Show your parlor tricks for the cheap gimmicks they are. I'll kill you before I allow you to beat me again. So this is your warning. You got lucky. Once. But nothing has changed. On this night, I will be the better man.

"Doll, you look ravishing in green. Don't you have a question for me?" He conceded the microphone to the interviewer.

She did not miss a beat. "Dmitri Petrovich, are you embracing a role as the villain?"

"And what? He is the hero!?! He's no hero. Two Hawks is the corruption of this sport. The outlook is bleak if he's your hero. He's a bad champion, and nobody likes him."

"Or maybe your loss has made you jealous?" It was hard to gauge his response behind the cracked skull mask.

"Number Eleven, you said you were serious. But you are just a number, and a buffoon at that. You're a disgrace to your religion, besides. You don't know how to be serious. But I'm deadly serious. If you step between me and this impostor, I will stamp your face into the ground."

"Stern words from the demonstrative Dmitri Petrovich."

Petrovich, who had just concluded his stomping gesture, grabbed Eleven's mirror shades off his face and threw them into the dirt.

With tremendous alacrity, the interviewer picked them up and intercepted Warhole Eleven before he could start a scuffle.

"My last question is for Artemeli. Baby, what are you going to buy me with your $100,000 win bonus?"

"Anything for you, baby girl. Thanks for the vote of confidence. Yeah, I'll buy you a Caribbean cruise."

"Ooooh, I can work on my tan."

He drew the microphone up to the mouth of his cheetah mask. "Quick message. For the whole world: peace!"

"Peace," she reiterated, looking dead into the camera's eye, an almost lewd beauty amid a rag-tag batch of barbarians, posturing around her malevolently.

*****

The camera cut to a ground shot, looking down at an angle at the crevice that opened into the Pit. It admitted Artemeli Skryke first—next, Warhole Eleven.

Seven million people were watching.

In spite of the scrap, Warhole Eleven's shades sat dead center. They reflected Skryke in his spotted leather cheetah mask. Skryke stood to defy all odds. He stalked his side of the Pit, breaking into fluttering jogs before turning and stalking the other way.

Their hidden gazes met, and, lifting their guards, the fight began. Thus, Pit FC 4 was initiated. The night to crown a champion.

Artemeli Skryke maintained the outer edge of the Pit, using his speed to elude Warhole Eleven's

PIT FC

clomping advancements. Eleven jabbed, then threw the straight cross, connecting with the cheetah's cheekbone. Skryke bobbed, then darted away. He came back with a pair of stabbing oblique kicks, aimed just north of Eleven's knee.

Warhole Eleven threw a gigantic front kick straight into the bracing arms of his opponent. Skryke was thrust back into the Pit's wall, losing his wind on impact. Eleven seemed to be channeling a side of his character we have yet to see: his anger. There was a ruthless edge to his attacks, a biting urgency.

He closed on Skryke, landing a right elbow to the forehead before pinning Skryke into the wall and beginning the bear down into him. Artemeli Skryke secured double underhooks, his hands locking around Eleven's torso above him. Warhole Eleven elevated himself with his left arm and came crashing down with another heavy right elbow to the crown of the head.

Skryke hit his knees, stunned, stupid, and waiting.

But Eleven stepped back and beckoned him to rise. He must've seen an opportunity on the feet. For his part, Skryke did not hesitate to reopen with a darting axe kick at Eleven's face. The aviators went soaring. A small cut opened under Eleven's left eye.

Warhole Eleven leveled out a volley of low-power punches to the ribs, sending shockwaves through Skryke's form. Artemeli Skryke ran away. His movement looked compromised.

Eleven loosed a short roar as he threw a high roundhouse at the head, which Skryke ducked, and Eleven spun through to his standard stance. He lowered his shoulder and threw a massive dig at Skryke's abdomen. Skryke folded but did not fall. Warhole Eleven overextended as he tried to follow Skryke down to the ground.

Skryke dug deep, lifting a scissoring upward knee to the underside of Eleven's chin. Eleven's eyes went blank for a split second while his brute form toppled onto his side, and, propping himself on one elbow, looking disorientated, he tried to stand back up.

Artemeli Skryke made a gliding dive for Eleven's head, cinching in a mounted guillotine, trying to tear his head off. Eleven didn't tap. Skryke stood up, raising his arms victoriously over the prostrate body of a limp and unconscious Warhole Eleven.

*****

The interviewer provided a break from the action. "I'm here with Juniper Jinn, who has some big news for us."

PIT FC

"Hi everybody. Sorry, you can't see me fight and win it all tonight. But I've got much bigger things in store. I'm pregnant!"

"That's so amazing! Congratulations! How did you find out?"

"A woman knows."

"And the father?"

"Warhole Eleven."

"I'm sorry you had to watch him lose."

"That's okay. I like him humble."

"I've got some rapid-fire fan questions for you. Are you ready?"

"Yes."

"An unknown talent?"

"Beer pong."

"Favorite color?"

"Pink."

"Favorite exercise?"

"Swimming."

"Favorite pet?"

"My fat cats."

"One word to describe Juniper Jinn?"

She stuttered over her words momentarily, then expressed, "Badass."

"How does a badass like yourself reflect back on Pit FC ten years from now?"

"I've always wanted to be a pit fighting champion. And I always knew I wanted to be a mother. Sadly, it was not in the cards for me to do both this year."

"Have we seen the last of Juniper Jinn?"

"No way, girl."

"Good. There are three fighters left standing in Pit FC. Who do you like to win?"

"None of them. But if I had to make a prediction: Two Hawks. He has powers."

"It has been an honor and a joy speaking with you the past few days. Do you have any final words for your audience?"

"The one thing they can't have is what will always keep them coming back. So never, ever give it to them."

*****

The stepping stones of experience beckon you on the path to pretty places of heart and spirit. You balance the moment in each step, surrender to patient revelation, and resolve to incandescent epiphany on the hinge of every choiceless goodbye. In the roaring silences in the corners of your eyes spent looking, there is a twin-

kling-like laughter. With just one more step, you move forward.

*****

Dmitri Petrovich was trying to give it to him. Artemeli Skryke still looked compromised, and the blood in the water drove Petrovich forward. In his unrivaled footwork, Skryke's cuts were ice cold, and his angles in and out varied and were sharp. But he seemed afraid to engage.

Remember, Petrovich was fast too. Like a cobra traversing the space between them, Petrovich's venom could be lethal if he could make contact. He led with a mega left hook, then caught Skryke by the hand and dragged the limb downward. With Skryke pulled off-balance, Petrovich thrust a sidekick up into his jaw. The cheetah mask, after bouncing back, appeared to hover in the air above his falling figure as he dropped onto his back left shoulder, rolled deftly onto the other shoulder, and used his momentum to catapult himself to his feet.

Two Two Hawks advanced toward him; he saw a double. But no, this was Petrovich, who for all his muscular brutality was lithe and avid in his movements, who was upon him like a cruel embrace, driving a knee into Skryke's gut.

Skryke stooped forward, Petrovich locked arms around him above the beltline, Skryke was lifted upside-down into the air, and Petrovich flung him halfway across the Pit into the wall. Skryke slid down, landing on his feet, balancing there, looking like a stubborn collection of bones that refused their rest. Skryke adjusted his limbs and escaped out of the path of Petrovich's impaling shoulder.

Now Petrovich moved as if enraged. Skryke's evasions were impressive as he dipped and dodged three consecutive punches. The fourth landed square on his forehead, staggering him.

Artemeli Skryke dived into a forward roll, came up before the wall, spun around, kicked off, and launched himself at Petrovich with a slicing elbow above the left eye. The skull mask separated decisively into two separate pieces and crumbled away to the ground.

Blind in one eye from a huge bleeding cut, Petrovich came forward. Skryke's jab pinged the cut again and again until it had opened so far that Petrovich's eye socket was halfway down his cheekbone and his cheek slunk around the jawline.

PIT FC

Dmitri Petrovich went down like a titan, swinging at the stars. He clutched his eye in one hand and fired wild but deadly hammers with the other. Skryke maintained his distance, and eventually Petrovich collapsed, drowning in his own blood.

Artemeli Skryke, spattered with some of that blood, lifted his arms in victory. The Bam Bam brothers rushed into the Pit to attend to Dmitri Petrovich.

*****

"The stage is set for our final fight. The phenomenal upstart Artemeli Skryke will showdown against undefeated provisional champion Two Hawks for the Pit FC's Grand Champion prize of $100,000. We're going to break for fifteen minutes. We'll be back with the main event!"

*****

Two Hawks perched in his narrow cot and applied his war paint. His thoughts were two hawks, soaring—made of menace, made of grace. He watched his dark and lovely visage hide behind a coat of white paint.

His stomach rumbled, and a metallic taste crept into the back of his mouth. But he would not eat before the fight.

He found himself distracted again by his thoughts of Juniper Jinn. He was jealous of the men who'd fought her. He was jealous of Warhole Eleven, who'd jostled her in the flesh.

He didn't feel threatened by the distraction. His thoughts could wander, for now. In the Pit, things changed.

He touched the scab above his eye. It was healing, for now.

He let the whites dry. Then he detailed the mask.

Sanctity is the act of building windows to let in the heavenly light. In this moment, we are given a window into the vulnerability of this invulnerable fighter, into the humanity of this superhuman contender. Before our eyes, Two Hawks is sanctified—an incarnation of magic.

He felt the heat in his chest as the sailing birds of his thoughts caught sight of their target, then felt a tingle somewhere else as he thought again of Jinn. She would not be impressed, even if he won it all. Even if he won it all. He sat there with the thought of sliding into her, and behind the mask of his cool demeanor, his thoughts were a cold frenzy of wings.

PIT FC

The sky opened, and light poured across his countenance, showing in vivid color the grain of his painted skin and the varying consistency of the paint. If he'd thought of her in that moment, was it she who brought the light?

He sealed the spell of paint with a dab of water.

*****

"The time is now. The culmination of four days of pit fighting is our main event. Is this the matchup you dreamed of, or has your contender already dashed his hopes? It all comes down to two men. Only their wills matter. Only their actions will count. As Pit FC passes into history, I assure you that the memories live on. Two Hawks versus Artemeli Skryke. The time is now."

It was apparent from the start that Skryke was a step faster. In the end, he had a step on everyone. In spite of this, he was apparently determined to stand in the pocket and trade.

Two Hawks popped him with the jab. He took a cross to the face. He popped the jab again. He slipped in a puddle of Petrovich's blood, and the fight went to the ground. He scrambled into top position, in Skryke's guard. As he tried to land punches, Skryke attacked the armbar, and he had to drive him into the ground and shake him off. Skryke threaded the needle with his legs and scooted back and up to his feet.

Skryke clobbered Two Hawks with a Superman punch. The cut on Two Hawks's forehead reopened and started trickling blood. Two Hawks unleashed a burst of energy—six alternating shots to the midriff. Skryke tried to engage the clinch, but Hawks shoved him back and landed a heavy right hand in the disengagement.

In the very center of the Pit, Two Hawks crouched down. The sound of a strange keening echoed around the Pit. Artemeli Skryke looked on. Two Hawks leaped up, fluttering his arms, levitating improbably, unleashing a flurry of kicks to Skryke's head and chest. It was terrifying. Two Hawks had achieved flight.

But in honesty, was he also perchance terrified that Skryke remained and refused to be dismissed? Or was he as unshakable as his record may have permitted?

As Two Hawks descended to the Pit floor, Artemeli Skryke crouched down, waited coiled, and pounced into a double leg that planted Two Hawks onto his back. He tried to make space for ground and pound action, but Hawks held him down by the back of the neck. Hawks dragged his arm across his body, got to a hip, and climbed up Skryke's exposed shoulder onto his back. Hawks clambered around him and dragged him backward, sliding in two hooks.

Hawks chopped at Skryke's temple and fought hands. Skryke was helpless to get his shoulders to the ground and try to peel him off. Hawks dragged him from side to side. "Don't get cocky," he whispered into Skryke's ear, and no one else heard.

Handfighting was paid to the account of Two Hawks. His rear naked choke was tight, and under the chin. His left forearm drove vertically into Skryke's back. For twenty seconds, he held the choke and squeezed. He lifted his arms up as if he'd won. He released the latch on his legs.

Skryke had been waiting, and when Hawks let go, he turned into him. He backed out of Hawks's guard, monitoring the feet for upkicks. Skryke moved in reverse, shapeshifting into a low crouch, a cat on all fours, ready to leap and bound.

If, as it seemed, it was fate that Two Hawks would prevail, then Skryke was undeterred in his vision to go down clawing and gnashing at the threads of the ineluctable.

He was spilling his guts into a narrative that ended in defeat, and when he saw it for what it was, he wondered in a timeless instant inside himself whether he wasn't too beat up, whether he wasn't just plain outmatched, whether he wanted to find a way out. Skryke snarled, the yellow fur of his nape bristling.

He was the Ace, and his posture in the arcanum of defeat was one of unremitting defiance. If Hijinks Olsen watched the fight somewhere, maybe he thought of the loons, and he would recognize the play of dominance and defiance in this crowning Pit FC event.

By seizing the upper hand in every situation, Two Hawks was breaking Skryke's will. Skryke found himself transfixed by an image of his demise, magnetized by its confounding sensibility and its harmonious relationship with the universe. Even the Ace could not save himself now, except that the Ace was pegged to a fabrication, and in his place was instinct.

On the other side, Two Hawks was on the verge of taking off, his bouncing steps hovering over the ground, as if gravity were letting up on his shackles. This was a showdown of elemental forces with animal proportions.

Two Hawks flew up again, and suddenly he was two, one form flipping backward and another ghostly avian form flipping forward, and both forms, man and raptor, swooped down upon Skryke's feral form. Brown feathers went bursting everywhere as Skryke swiped a paw at the winged form of Hawks's double. The feathers evanesced into flower petals drifting pinkly in the spectral air around these two men, men once again.

Two Hawks yanked the dangling ear clear off his own skull and discarded it to the side without a sense of loss. He was moving forward at any cost.

Two Hawks dropped a knee and shot at Skryke. The two men grappled against the Pit wall, exchanging underhooks like hugs between brothers.

When Two Hawks slipped free, the fight seemed to reset into the mode in which it began, with Hawks and Skryke exchanging blows in the pocket, now at a noticeable uptick in intensity.

Sweat and blood sprayed luridly off the two fighters.

At the height of inspiration and to the maximum of brevity, Two Hawks blew Artemeli a kiss, timing it between blows. It was a slugfest, and Two Hawks ended it with a powerful straight through the jaw. Skryke went down swinging.

All reasons fail at the point of pressure, which breaks them. For Artrmeli Skryke's championship aspirations, that point of pressure was his jaw. In this final instance of Pit FC, the man who called himself the Ace fell before the one who was two.

Two Hawks turned away, muttering "You got cocky," for absolutely no one to hear, and fanned out his wingspan in a gesture of absolute victory. Skryke lifted a hand as the figure receded, but he let it drop. Knockout victory for Grand Champion Two Hawks.

With the interviewer, he was overcome by the unquenchable urge to speak his own true name in that instant. He knew he couldn't, and it passed like an unrelieved itch into pain and then forgetting.

"Two Hawks, you are the Pit FC Grand Champion. What do you like more, the title or the money?"

"I'll take the $100,000. I already know who I am."

"In an already legendary career, 17–0, where does this rank among your previous wins?"

"This has to be number one."

"What makes Artemeli Skryke such a great opponent?"

"The same thing—and this is not true of everyone—but for Skryke, it is the same as it is for me. It's mystery. Only when you watch can you see."

The interviewer gasped and said, "The walls are shaking." She dropped the microphone.

They ran for the ramp, but to nine million live viewers, it looked like it was too late for them. They vanished amid the falling earth, and the last thing anyone saw of Pit FC was the roof collapsing. The final determination of fate for those two was inconclusive, but the look was sufficiently bad.

All the spammed "RIP Two Hawks" comments over the past four days took on a sad and painful irony.

The cycles of return, they had found their moment in the soil, that potent darkness, and in the slap of a cataclysmic hand, he had found himself engulfed in the soil, the resonance of remembrance, an incandescent influx of mortal terror amidst underground's eternal night; and within the sigh of inevitability, he found the cry that rails against all finality.

The Pit had swallowed its greatest champion. The enigmatic Two Hawks had returned to earth, the flutter of his four wings forever silenced in the damp embrace of the Mother. Or not.

The Pit regurgitated him. Rather, he clawed his way out of the fucker's throat. The first thing that no one saw of Two Hawks that night in the dark wood above a forgotten hole in the ground was his arm emerging from a tumult of earth. Two Hawks's hand closed into a fist. Still undefeated.

"Strait is the gate, brothers," Warhole Eleven elsewhere said. "Never did get that rematch."

About the Author

Brenden Haukos lives in central Minnesota. His previous books are *The Power of Positive Imagery* and *Sparkly Cakes and Cinnamon Swirls.*

www.ingramcontent.com/pod-product-compliance
Lightning Source LLC
LaVergne TN
LVHW091455130525
811150LV00030B/278